GOD'S TRUTH FOR YOU

ISBN 978-1-63814-093-1 (Paperback)
ISBN 978-1-63814-095-5 (Hardcover)
ISBN 978-1-63814-094-8 (Digital)

Covenant Books, Inc.
11661 Hwy 707
Murrells Inlet, SC 29576
www.covenantbooks.com

GOD'S TRUTH FOR YOU

Sarah Ensing

"Goodnight Beautiful" Mama said as she tucked PeeWee in after their bedtime prayers.

"Mama, can you tell me about God?" PeeWee stated.

Mama replied, "I can tell you what God says about you!"

"Yes!" PeeWee shouted.

"Well Alright, scoot your tail feather over so we can cuddle."

"You are fearfully and wonderfully made." "Made by who?" questioned Pee Wee.

"You are God's Creation, He made the world and everything in it; including you."

Psalm 139:14
Genesis 1

"Did he make my favorite blanket?"

Mama laughed "Of course he did. He created the person that made your blanket and then they used their talent to make your blanket."

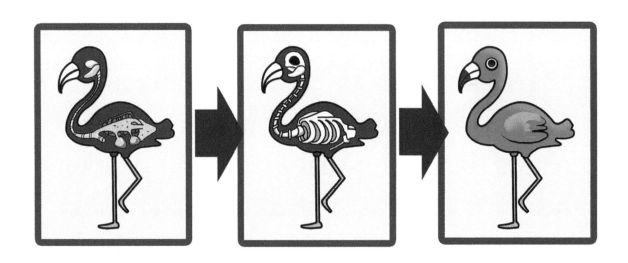

"Just like you think that blanket is made perfectly, you are made perfectly. You are perfect on the inside and on the outside. You are special and unique."

"What is unique?" asked PeeWee.
"Mhmm", Mama replied, unique means
you are one of a kind. No one is the same,
and that is what makes this world so fun."

Psalm 139:15

"How does God have enough love for me and the whole world?", asked PeeWee. "God's love is endless and unconditional." "Uncondic-what?" questioned PeeWee.

John 3:16,
Romans 8:38-39

"Mama and Daddy love you no matter what you do or say, right?"

"Right!" PeeWee answered.

"Well God also loves you no matter what forever and ever. Did you know you can show God's love to others?"

"No, I did not know that", replied PeeWee.

"When you help your little brother find his toy, or when you bake cookies for the neighborhood ducks, you are using your talent that God gave you. They will be able to feel your love and God's love for them."

Ephesians 2:10

17

"Mama, did you know that you are my best friend?", yawned PeeWee.

"I love being your best friend! God is also your best friend", replied Mama as she pulled the blankets up around PeeWee's neck.

"God is always with you and you can talk to him about anything", Mama said as she turned off the overhead light.

PeeWee sat straight up in bed, "Mama, don't forget my nightlight, sometimes I get scared."

John 15:5

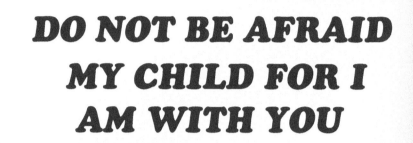

Then a whisper came into PeeWees little ear, "Do Not Be Afraid My Child For I Am With You". PeeWee just smiled and laid back down. "Goodnight Mama, I love you."

Joshua 1:9

"Goodnight my love, I pray you always remember You are kind, important, strong, beautiful, and smart. You are very precious to me. I love you and God loves you."

About the Author

Sarah is a Michigan native and a first-time author to "God's Truth For You". She loves embarking on new adventures with her husband, Cody and their two children. She loves enjoying God's creation in nature with her two Labrador retrievers. Sarah also has a heart to help others and works as a registered nurse at a local hospital. In her free time, she enjoys crafting, hunting, and volunteering. One of her favorite activities is spending time with God. She is very thankful for the many blessings God has entrusted to her. Her biggest hope for this book is that it will help you raise the children in your life to know they belong to God and He loves them unconditionally.

CPSIA information can be obtained
at www.ICGtesting.com
Printed in the USA
LVHW071116220222
711715LV00015B/822

9 781638 140931